Infinite LEGO

Infinite LEGO

Ryan M Blanck

Infinite LEGO

Ryan M Blanck

Reimagining David Foster Wallace's
Infinite Jest through LEGO

ISBN Color Edition: 978-1-943170-12-8

ISBN Black and White Edition: 978-1-943170-13-5

All Images: Ryan M Blanck

Cover and Interior Design: Jane L Carman

Typeface: Arial

Published by: Lit Fest Press

Carman

688 Knox Road 900 North

Gilson, Illinois 61436

There are no rules.

festivalwriter.org

To Dave. Thanks for everything.

Acknowledgements

I wish to acknowledge the contributions of the following people:

Tanya, Emma, and Morgan, for their endless support, encouragement, and patience of my creative endeavors.

Jane L Carman and the staff of Lit Fest Press, for giving me this opportunity to share my artwork.

Introduction

It all began on a date night with my wife a couple of years back. We live in a rather boring town, and money was kind of tight, so after a relatively inexpensive dinner at our favorite pizza place we went to browse the aisles of our local Barnes & Noble. We happened upon *The Brick Bible* by Brendan Smith and loved the concept—the entire Biblical narrative retold in graphic novel form, but with the images being LEGO sculptures. Feeling inspired, we enlisted the help of our daughters to launch our own LEGO Bible blog. We got through the book of Genesis and part way through Exodus before the project sputtered and fell by the wayside.

A couple of years later, I was working on my proposal for a paper the first annual David Foster Wallace Conference hosted by Illinois State University, and I gave a second read to the "Original Creative Works" call for submissions. Then a thought came to me.

"I like David Foster Wallace," I thought.

"I like LEGOs," I thought.

"So, why not bring those two together," I thought.

I selected some of my favorite scenes from some of my favorite stories, and I began to build. Scenes from "Little Expressionless Animals," "Forever Overhead," and "Good People;" along with scenes from the novels: *Broom of the System*, *Infinite Jest*, and *The Pale King*. Even one taken from "This is Water." I built the sculptures and photographed them and assembled the images into a digital slideshow. Then it was off to Bloomington-Normal for the Conference.

At the Conference, I was honored to be selected as a featured panelist for my "Reimagining Wallace" presentation. Then I was shocked to see such a large crowd gathered to view my creations on the very large screen. I did not expect pictures of LEGOs to be such a hit at an academic conference.

Inspired by the positive response to my presentation, I went home and continued building more Wallace-inspired LEGO sculptures, now focusing my attention on his magnum opus, *Infinite Jest* (Go big or go home, am I right?). As my understanding and enjoyment of Dave's writings continue to evolve, so do my artistic expressions that he inspires. What I love about Dave's writing is that it not only invites serious academic consideration, but that it also invites and inspires creative response. In my case, that has included blog posts, imitative essays, and now LEGO creations. Who knows what will be next...

Author's Note

In attempting to tackle the monumental challenge of recreating *Infinite Jest* in LEGO sculptures, I quickly faced the conundrum of how to organize and present the art; how to order this book. I decided, rather than attempting a chronological or chapter-by-chapter ordering, I would group the images thematically. We start at Enfield Tennis Academy and end down the hill at Ennet House, making a few side trips along the way.

Additionally, creations are not exact representations of the text. In many instances, I took some creative license to convey the spirit of the text rather than the letter of it (and to have a little fun while I build).

Infinite LEGO

Ryan M Blanck

Section 1: Enfield Tennis Academy

Hal's Admission Interview at University of Arizona

The novel begins at the chronological end of the story, Hal's admission interview at the University of Arizona. Hal is surrounded by his own entourage, including Charles Tavis and his mother, Avril Incandenza, as well as a number of deans from the U of A. The already tense and awkward interview takes a huge turn for the worse when Hal opens his mouth to answer some questions.

Hal's Admission Interview at University of Arizona

Hal Remembers Eating Fungus

During his admissions interview, Hal's mind wanders off to the child-hood memory of the time he ate a strange fungus that he found out in the yard.

Hal Remembers Eating Fungus

Hal & Don Gately Dig up JOI's Grave

Another passing memory as Hal sits in the Dean of Admission's office is the time he and Don Gately dug up James Incandenza's grave presumably in hopes of finding the missing video cartridge of *The Entertainment*.

Hal & Don Gately Dig up JOI's Grave

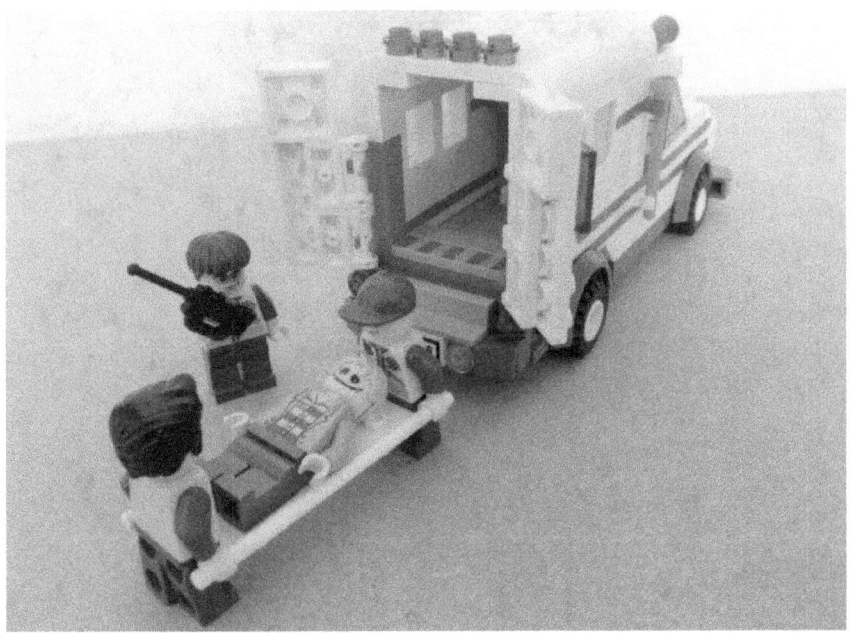

Hal Taken Away in an Ambulance

The interview goes horribly wrong as strange noises start coming out of Hal's mouth when he tries to talk. Hal is wrestled to the floor and carted away in an ambulance.

Hal & The Conversation Specialist

Prior to his death, James "Himself" Incandenza disguises himself as a professional conversationalist in order to uncover the reason his son, Hal, won't speak to him.

Hal Smokes in the ETA Basement

Hal is a pothead. One of his favorite places to get high is in the labyrinthine basement of Enfield. The complex air circulation system allows the smoke to dissipate and his addiction to go undetected.

Hal & Mario Talk about JOI's death

One evening shortly after Himself's funeral, Hal and Mario lie awake talking about their father.

Orin & the Dead Bird

While talking with his younger brother, Hal, Orin sees a dead bird fall into the nearby hot tub.

Orin Parachutes into the Stadium

As part of the Cardinals' pregame festivities, Orin parachutes into the stadium wearing a bird costume.

Orin Practices Kicking Field Goals

A virtual novice at the game of football, Orin surprises coaches with his ability to punt and kick nearly record-setting field goals.

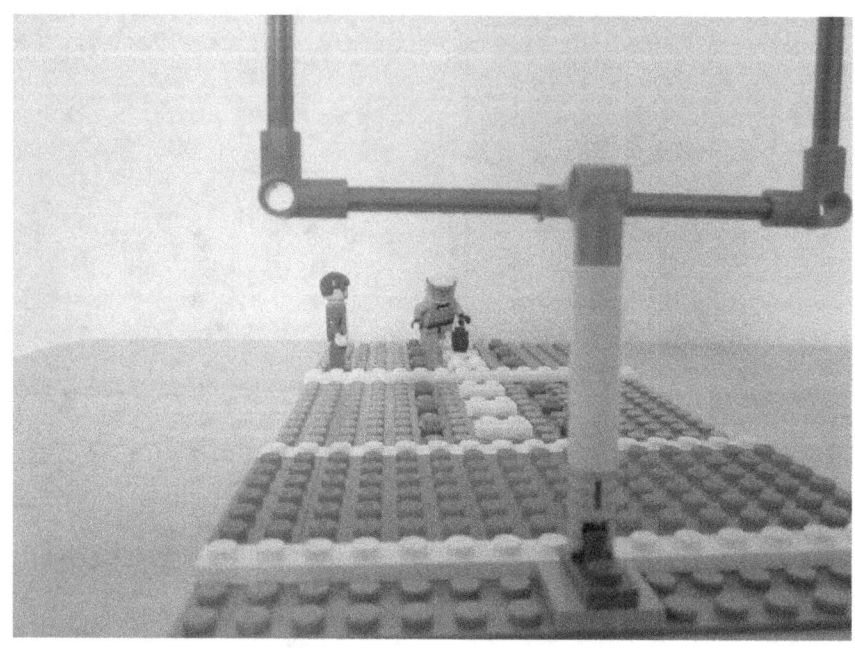

Orin Practices Kicking Field Goals

JOI & His Dad Talk Outside the Garage

Young James Incandenza has a father-son moment with his father as they talk about tennis, Marlon Brando, and the father's own tennis injury.

JOI's Suicide

Just as mysterious as the reasons he took his own life is the method James Incandenza chose to carry out this final act: sticking his head in a microwave. It was Hal who discovered the grisly sight.

JOI's Suicide

Mario & Schtitt Talk Tennis and Life

Mario rides along with Schtitt as the tennis players go for their workout run. As the players practice on the courts, Schtitt shares with Mario his philosophy of both tennis and life.

Mario & Schtitt Talk Tennis and Life

Mario's First Ever Romantic Encounter

Mario is chased into a field by the "USS" Millicent Kent, who accosts him and puts her hand down his pants, giving Mario his first and only even remotely romantic experience.

Mario's Film "This is How To…"

Mario produces a film as an orientation to new Enfield students. Starring Hal, the film introduces newcomers to the ins and outs of the Tennis Academy.

Mario's Film "This is How To..."

Michael Pemulis and Hal Talk with Their Little Buddies

Each upperclassman at ETA is assigned a group of younger students to mentor and advise in tennis, academics, and life. Michael Pemulis and Hal Incandenza share nuggets of wisdom with their little buddies.

Michael Pemulis and Hal Talk with Their Little Buddies

In the Locker Room

After a hard workout on the tennis courts, the guys hang out in the locker room.

In the Locker Room

Lyle Dispenses His Wisdom

Lyle, an enigmatic, sweat-licking guru, sits in the boys' locker room, giving advice to anyone who will listen or enquire.

Drug Testing Day

Many of the students at ETA use a variety of illicit drugs, but also face routine drug testing. In order to avoid getting caught, the dopers and the druggies buy clean urine samples from Pemulis who buys samples from a few of the young'uns who abstain from using drugs for the purpose of making money.

Drug Testing Day

Drug Testing Day

Tennis Matches

The student athletes of Enfield Tennis Academy take on rival school,
Port Washington Tennis Academy.

Tennis Matches

Tennis Matches

Tennis Matches

The Bus Ride

The student athletes celebrate their latest tennis victory on the bus ride back to ETA.

The Bus Ride

Tennis Match with Gun

Exhibition tennis player, Eric Clipperton, plays his matches while pointing a gun to his own head, threatening to kill himself if he loses.

Tennis Match with Gun

Eschaton

One of the traditions at Enfield Tennis Academy is Eschaton, a highly sophisticated war simulation game played across the tennis courts. Students lob tennis balls, representing nuclear warheads, at strategic targets in other players' territories. The gamemaster, Otis P Lord, calculates the damage from each hit. But things get out of hand as one player throws a ball directly at an opponent, breaking game protocol and instigating an all-out brawl on the courts.

Eschaton

Eschaton

Mario's Film "The Formation of ONAN"

On Interdependence Day, Mario shows his feature-length documentary film about the formation of ONAN to a captivated crowd.

Mario's Film "The Formation of ONAN"

Mario's Film "The Formation of ONAN"

Hal at the NA Meeting

Hal goes to what he thinks is a Narcotics Anonymous meeting, but it turns out to be a psychotherapy group session focusing on one's Inner Infant.

Hal at the NA Meeting

Hal at the NA Meeting

Infinite LEGO

Ryan M Blanck

Section 2: *The Entertainment*

Medical Attache Watches *The Entertainment*

Somehow a Medical Attache, the personal physician of a Near Eastern dignitary, winds up with *The Entertainment* video cartridge in his possession. Wanting to enjoy a relaxing evening, he unwittingly starts watching the cartridge—the last thing he will ever do.

Medical Attache Watches *The Entertainment*

Older Medical Attache Watches *The Entertainment*

The Medical Attache continues to watch *The Entertainment*.

Older Medical Attache Watches *The Entertainment*

The Medical Attache continues watching *The Entertainment*.

Dead Medical Attache Watches *The Entertainment*

The Entertainment continues to play as the Medical Attache, now dead, continues to watch.

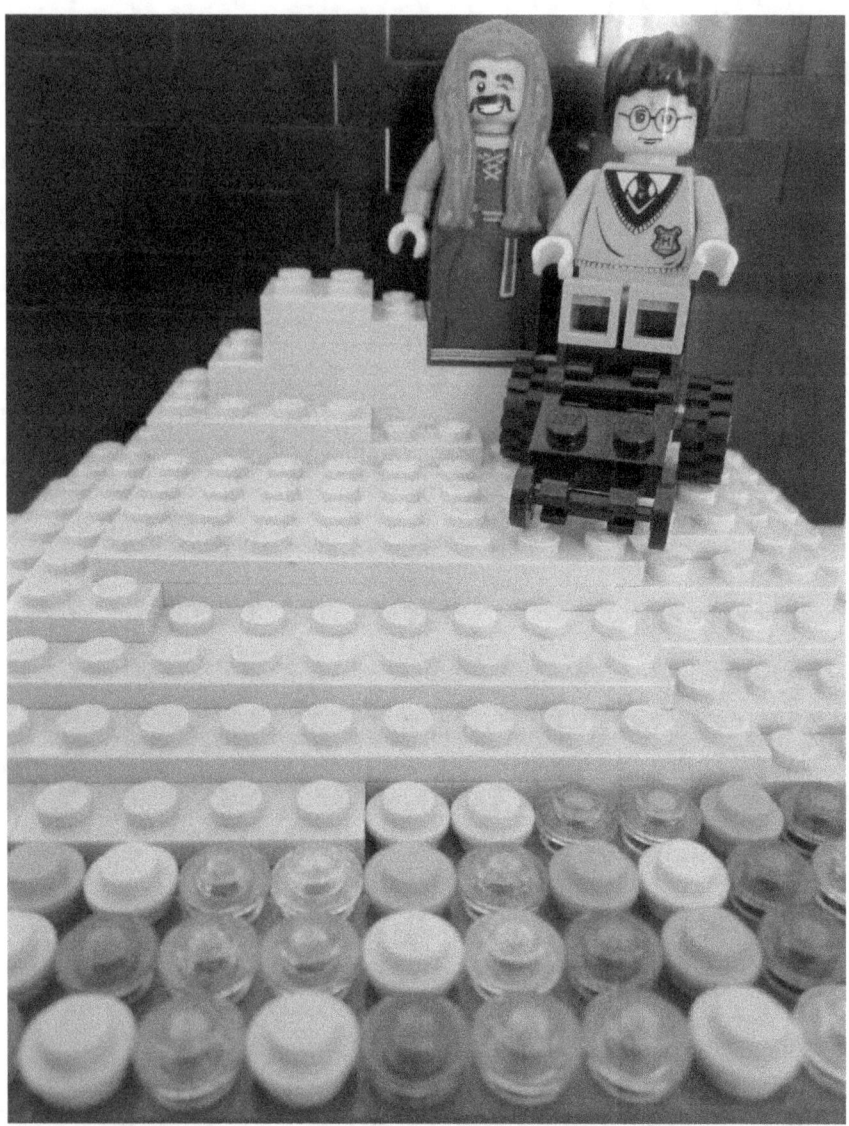

Marathe & Steeply

Much like the chorus in a Greek play, Marathe and Steeply stand on a hillside overlooking Tucson, AZ. Both are double - and maybe even triple - agents as they discuss the possible location of the lost video cartridge containing the master copy of *The Entertainment*, a film that is so addictive that the viewer quite literally cannot stop watching it.

The Wheelchair Assassins

The Wheelchair Assassins descend on a Boston-area video store looking for *The Entertainment*.

The Wheelchair Assassins

Infinite LEGO

Ryan M Blanck

Section 3: Other Storylines

Subsidized Time

In the not-so-distant semi-dystopian future, the very calendar has been subjugated to corporate sponsorship. On January 1 of each year, the product sponsoring the new year is placed atop the torch held by the Statue of Liberty.

Subsidized Time

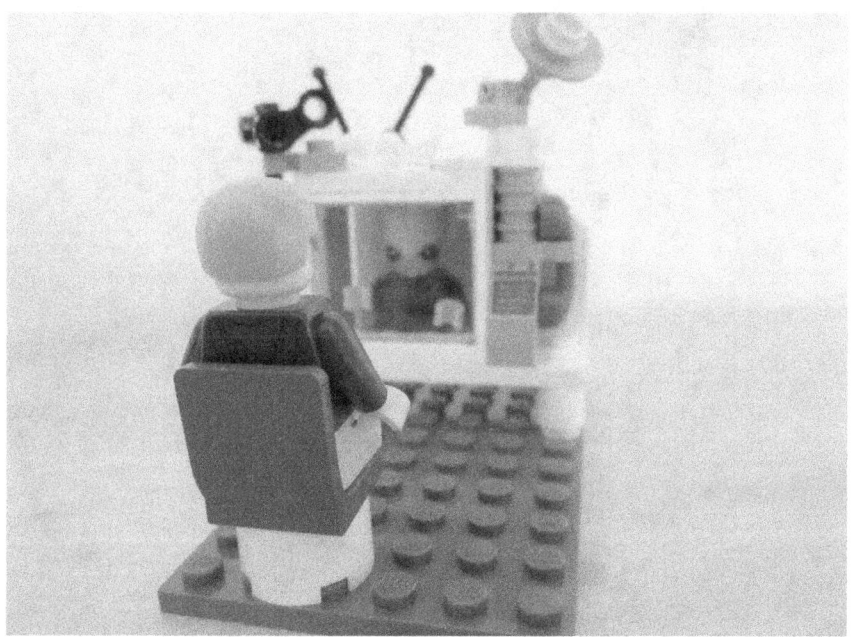

The Videophone

Advances in technology now allow people to see the person they are speaking to on the phone. However, this causes people a great deal of anxiety and self-consciousness as they worry about how they appear on the screen.

The Videophone

The Feral Hamsters

Originating from the Great Concavity, a horde of feral hamsters is on the move throughout North America, causing fear in anyone who comes across them.

The Feral Hamsters

The Great Concavity

A Great Concavity, a vast barren wasteland, now exists on the border of Canada and the United States. Huge catapults have been constructed to launch trash into the Concavity.

The Bricklayer's Accident

A bricklayer files an insurance claim after an unfortunate accident on the job site. Holding onto a rope attached through a pulley to a large bucket of bricks, he is hoisted off the ground. His hand first gets caught in the pulley above, then he plunges toward the ground as bricks fall out of the bucket, offsetting the weight balance. On his way down, he is struck by the bucket of bricks on its way up. After finally letting go of the rope, the bucket plummets to the ground, landing on the poor bricklayer.

The Bricklayer's Accident

Madame Psychosis

Joelle—the Prettiest Girl Of All Time, star of *The Entertainment*, former love interest of Orin Incandenza, and graduate of Ennet House—assumes the persona of Madame Psychosis and hosts a night time radio program that is especially popular among young men.

Infinite LEGO

Ryan M Blanck

Section 4: Ennet House

Ennet House Exterior

Ennet House is a halfway house for recovering addicts. The building is part of a larger complex that was once Enfield Marine VA Hospital. It is home to Don Gately, Tiny Ewell, Kate Gompert, Poor Tony Krause, and others.

Ennet House Exterior

Ennet House Interior

In the Ennet House common room, Don Gately lounges on the couch while others discuss their respective stages of recovery.

Ken Erdedy Waits for the Woman to Bring Him Drugs

Ken Erdedy, a future resident of Ennet House, plans on one last dope-binge weekend, wanting to make himself so sick that he never wants to try the drugs again. The woman who is supposed to deliver the dope is late, and Erdedy is in a panic. His anxiety reaches a climax when the phone and doorbell ring simultaneously; Erdedy is frozen, not sure which one to answer.

Don Gately Gets Arrested

Don Gately, a petty thief and drug addict, burglarizes houses to support his drug habit. A house he presumes to be empty isn't, so he binds
and gags the homeowner while he robs him. Gately doesn't know that
the homeowner has a horrible head cold and can no longer breathe
because of the gag in his mouth. The homeowner dies, and Gately is
charged in his death.

Don Gately Gets Arrested

Kate Gompert on Suicide Watch

Kate Gompert lies in a hospital bed after her latest suicide attempt. Severely depressed, she requests electro-shock therapy or hard drugs from the young resident who has no idea how to handle this extreme case.

Tiny Ewell & the Cab

Tiny Ewell is transported by taxi to Ennet House to continue his recovery. While there, he becomes obsessed with analyzing and categorizing his housemates' tattoos.

Tiny Ewell & the Cab

Tony Krause Steals a Woman's Heart

Poor Tony Krause, dressed in drag, snatches a woman's purse and takes off running down the street. Unbeknownst to P.T. Krause, the purse contains the woman's artificial heart. As he runs off, the woman cries out, 'She stole my heart! She stole my heart!' Unfortunately, bystanders don't realize she isn't speaking metaphorically.

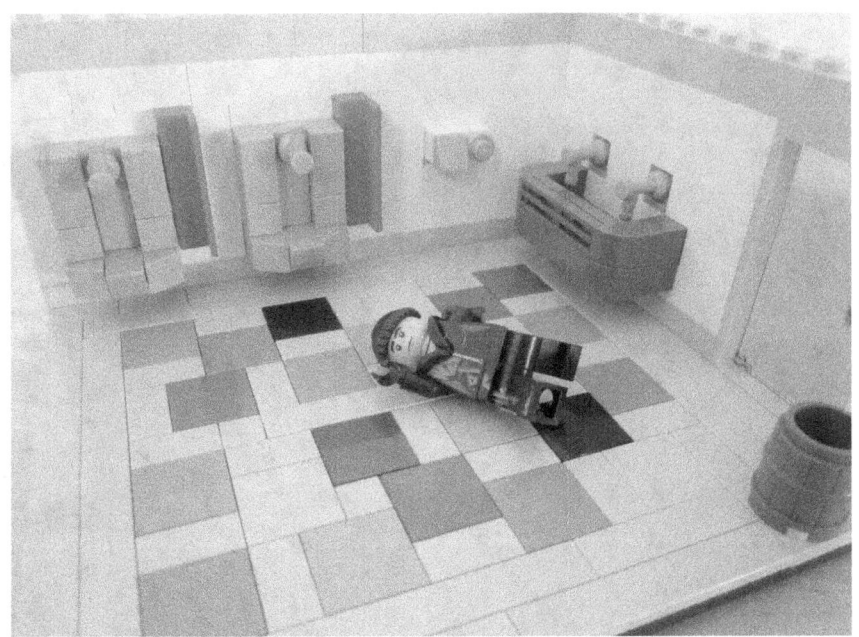

Tony Krause in Detox

Poor Tony Krause experiences intense withdrawal symptoms while in the bathroom at the public library.

Tony Kraus on the Train

Poor Tony Krause experiences a full-blown seizure while riding the public transit train.

Joelle Attempts to Overdose

At a party for cinema grad students, Joelle attempts to overdose in the bathroom.

Randy Lenz

Randy Lenz is a troubled resident of Ennet House. He releases his pent up frustration by catching feral cats in a bag, then smashing the bag down on the sidewalk, shouting, "There!" as he does it.

Don Gately Cleans the Bathroom

Don Gately works a job outside of Ennet House, cleaning the restrooms of a nearby establishment.

Don Gately Prays to a God of His Own Making

Although he is an atheist, Don Gately knows that the methods and ideology of AA work. So every morning and evening he gets down on his knees to pray to a god of his own making for the strength to remain sober for another day.

Don Gately Prays to a God of His Own Making

AA Meetings

AA Meetings are a staple of the lives of the residents of Ennet House; most go to meetings several times per week. The guest speakers share the often graphic details of their stories of addiction and recovery.

AA Meetings

AA Meetings

The Shootout

A confrontation out in front of Ennet House erupts into gunfire. Don Gately gets in the middle of things, trying to break up the fight (and kicking a little ass in the process of defending the helpless Randy Lenz), but ends up getting caught in the crossfire. He is rushed to the hospital to be treated for his gunshot wound.

The Shootout

The Shootout

The Shootout

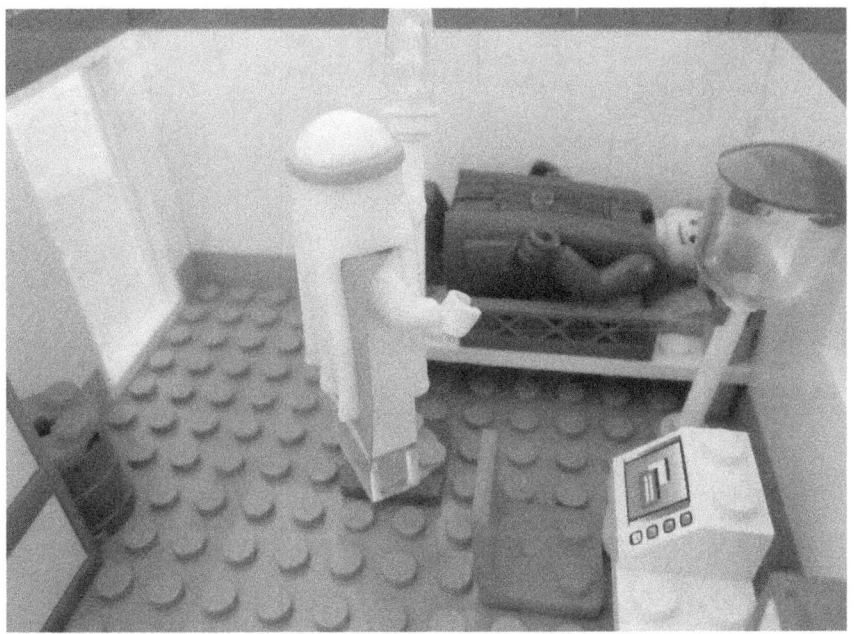

Don Gately in the Hospital

Don Gately fights for his life as he attempts to recover from his gun-shot wound. He endures excruciating pain, not wanting to take any pain medication for fear of becoming addicted again. He is visited by a Wraith (possibly the ghost of James Incandenza) while in his hospital bed. His refusal to take the pain meds, even if doing so might cost him his life, helps him to emerge victorious in this final battle against his addiction.

Don Gately in the Hospital

Don Gately in the Hospital

The End

Infinite LEGO

Ryan M Blanck

David Foster Wallace as minifigure

Infinite LEGO

Ryan M Blanck

David Foster Wallace in LEGO pixels

About the Author

Ryan M Blanck is a high school English teacher and writer from Southern California. He has written extensively about David Foster Wallace on his blog, Letters to DFW. He presented critical and creative works at the Work in Process conference in Antwerp, Belgium, and at the DFW Conference at Illinois State University. Ryan has written and published six books, including *Supposedly Fun Things*, a collection of essays inspired by the creative nonfiction of Wallace. Ryan hopes to continue his LEGO building by reimagining DFW's other works in LEGO sculptures.

Infinite LEGO

Ryan M Blanck